"A weird story." —*The Literary World*

"*The Yellow Wallpaper* is a literary gem and ranks with Poe's best work."   —*The Minneapolis Journal*

"Charlotte Perkins Gilman's greatest literary achievement . . . a landmark feminist work and an important contribution to the American literary canon."
                              —*Twentieth-Century Literary Criticism*

"Rises to a classic level in subtly." —H.P. Lovecraft

"That strange study of physical environment, *The Yellow Wallpaper*, deservedly ranks as one of the most powerful of American short stories."   —*Current Literature*

"Deceptively simple."
—Loralee MacPike, *American Literary Realism 1870-1910*

"Grows and increases with a perfect crescendo of horror . . . The story is simple, serious, sly, fascinating, torturing. It is embodied excitement. It is brooding insanity."
                              —Anne Montgomerie, *Conservator*

"A striking example of unadulterated pessimism in book form is *The Yellow Wallpaper*, which is quite hair-raising and as creepy as even the most perverted imagination could desire to feed upon."   —*The Richmond Times-Dispatch*

"[A] remarkable study in progressive mania . . . It is a gruesome, but wonderfully strong and vivid little story . . . But unless the publishers of the book wish to be responsible for a large crop of maniacs, they ought not to have covered it with what is apparently a reproduction of that fateful wallpaper. After one glance at its pattern, one cannot wonder that the poor woman went crazy." —*The Los Angeles Times*

I never saw so much expression in an inanimate thing before . . .

The Yellow Wallpaper
Charlotte Perkins Gilman

HEATHEN SHORTS
THEIR STORIES. OUR WAY.

Published in the good ole United States of America
by Heathen Shorts, an imprint of
Heathen Creative
P.O. Box 588
Point Pleasant, WV 25550-0588

Heathen Shorts are available at quantity discounts.
Bear witness to the yackety-yak and tomfoolery at:

heatheneditions.com

Social? Tag us! @heatheneditions
Photo? Tag it! #heathenedition #heathenshort

Caution: This book may alter your mind.

"Perilous Stuff" published in *Boston Evening Transcript* April 8, 1892

"She Walketh Veiled and Sleeping" published in *In This Our World* 1893

"The Yellow Wall-paper" first published in
The New England Magazine January 1892

Published as "The Yellow Wall Paper" 1899

"Why I Wrote The Yellow Wallpaper?" published in
The ForeRunner October 1913

Heathen Short published December 17, 2025

Book and cover design by Sheridan Cleland
Set in 11pt Sabon LT Std
Titles in Belisa Plumilla Manual

ISBN: 979-8-90075-001-9

**HEATHEN SHORT #1
FIRST EDITION**

Contents

PERILOUS STUFF.

To the Editor of the Transcript: In a well-known magazine has recently appeared a story entitled "The Yellow Wall-Paper." It is a sad story of a young wife passing through the gradations from slight mental derangement to raving lunacy. It is graphically told, in a somewhat sensational style, which makes it difficult to lay it aside, after the first glance, till it is finished, holding the reader in morbid fascination to the end. It certainly seems open to serious question if such literature should be permitted in print.

The story can hardly, it would seem, give pleasure to any reader, and to many, whose lives have been touched through the nearest ties by this dread disease, it must bring the keenest pain. To others, whose lives have become a struggle against an heredity of mental derangement, such literature contains deadly peril. Should such stories be allowed to pass without protest, without severest censure?

M. D.

BOSTON EVENING TRANSCRIPT.
FRIDAY, APRIL 8, 1892.

She Walketh Veiled and Sleeping

She walketh veiled and sleeping,
For she knoweth not her power;
She obeyeth but the pleading
Of her heart, and the high leading
Of her soul, unto this hour.
Slow advancing, halting, creeping,
Comes the Woman to the hour!—
She walketh veiled and sleeping,
For she knoweth not her power.

HEATHENRY
Thoughts on the Text

To hyphen or not to hyphen, that is the question . . .

First published in the January 1892 edition of *The New England Magazine*[1] as "The Yellow Wall-paper" (with hyphen) and bearing her first married name — Charlotte Perkins Stetson[2] — this story arrives with a title whose hyphen has a history all its own.

We call attention to it only because, while we've chosen the modern form in keeping with our standard Heathening procedure — wallpaper (without hyphen) — we also acknowledge the symbolic duality unlocked when the hyphen is present: wall-paper.

That hyphen isn't decoration; it's a wound. It splits *wall* from *paper*, revealing both the barrier that cages our narrator and the material that taunts her.

Follow the duality further and the wall becomes two things at once: literal, in that it confines her, and figurative, in that she is pressed against a wall of disconnection and misunderstanding erected by those who profess to heal her. And yes, the hideous paper clinging to that wall is a literal

---

[1] A monthly literary magazine published in Boston, Massachusetts, by J. N. McClinctock and Company from 1884 to 1917.

[2] Charlotte was married to American artist Charles Walter Stetson (1858–1911) from 1884 until their amicable divorce in 1894.

material — but it is also figurative in that material can be facts, information, and ideas. You know, the same "facts, information, and ideas" that convinced those around her that a "rest cure" was medicine rather than a sentence.

It's no wonder this story has endured for as long as it has, the layers of wisdom to be mined are immense. Enough so that one would think its hyphen usage has been consistent since its first publication, yet alas . . .

[stats for nerds]

In its first appearance in 1892 in *The New England Magazine*, the word is hyphenated in the title and five other places, but presented as one word five times.

Then, in its first book appearance, in the 1899 Small, Maynard & Company edition, the hyphen is jettisoned completely in favor making it two words throughout: wall paper.

To confound further, Gilman herself favors one word entirely when referring to the story in her "Why I Wrote The Yellow Wallpaper?" published in the October 1913 edition of her magazine *The ForeRunner*, (which we have included as an epilogue, of sorts).

[/stats for nerds]

Do these stats matter? With or without hyphen, we believe the implication is the same: the wallpaper is a prison.

Perhaps, though, the most interesting thing we've discovered about this story is a fascinating contradiction.

First, backstory: by the 1970s, Gilman's work had fallen into obscurity. Then, Elaine Ryan Hedges[3] wrote an afterword for the 1973 Feminist Press chapbook of "The Yellow Wall-Paper" (with hyphen) and called Gilman "one of the most commanding feminists of her time."

---

[3] Elaine Ryan Hedges (1927–1997) was an American feminist and recognized expert in feminist literary criticism, who pioneered Women's Studies in the 1970s and advocated for curricula encompassing a more inclusive body of American literature which brought together works by ethnic and gendered minorities.

That edition essentially resurrected Gilman's work, and became a key text for feminist courses throughout the country.

But, here's the contradiction: Gilman never saw herself as a feminist. In a letter she wrote, "I abominate being called a feminist."[4]

"Gilman insisted she was not a feminist; rather the world was 'mascunilist'"[5] — potato, potahto? — but that tracks considering Gilman is credited with inventing the term "masculism" in 1914, when she gave a public lecture series in New York entitled "Studies in Masculism."[6]

Regardless, we Heathens have realized we'd never want to squabble with Gilman: her words were weapons.

Now, as for the text, in addition to the wallpaper hyphen, we have eliminated some others so as to render them modern (to-day is today, to-morrow is tomorrow, and so on).

As a bonus to "Why I Wrote The Yellow Wallpaper?" we've included a facsimile of the "protest" Gilman mentions so you can judge it yourself.

Opposite that, you'll find Gilman's 1893 poem "She Walketh Veiled and Sleeping" as we believe it pairs well with this *material*.

We've also appended 29 footnotes to enhance your reading of the text, and to provide clarity, context, and commentary where necessary.

In all, we're quite pleased with how well our first **Heathen Short** has come together, and believe there's only one word that can accurately describe it: bitchin' — ♥!

---

[4] Butler, H. (2021, March 11). The Trouble with Charlotte Perkins Gilman. *The Paris Review.* theparisreview.org/blog/2021/03/11/the-trouble-with-charlotte-perkins-gilman

[5] Lane, A. J. (1980). The Fictional World of Gilman. *The Charlotte Perkins Gilman Reader*, p. xiv.

[6] Allen, J. A. (2009). Woman Suffrage, the Antis, and Masculism. *The Feminism of Charlotte Perkins Gilman: Sexualities, Histories, Progressivism*, p. 152.

Here is a little
Nightmare —

The Yellow Wallpaper

It is very seldom that mere ordinary people like John and myself secure ancestral halls for the summer.

A colonial mansion, a hereditary estate, I would say a haunted house, and reach the height of romantic felicity[1] — but that would be asking too much of fate!

Still I will proudly declare that there is something queer about it.

Else, why should it be let so cheaply? And why have stood so long untenanted?

John laughs at me, of course, but one expects that in marriage.

John is practical in the extreme. He has no patience with faith, an intense horror of superstition, and he scoffs openly at any talk of things not to be felt and seen and put down in figures.

John is a physician, and *perhaps* — (I would not say it to a living soul, of course, but this is dead paper and a great relief to my mind) — *perhaps* that is one reason I do not get well faster.

You see, he does not believe I am sick!

---

[1] Intense happiness.

And what can one do?

If a physician of high standing, and one's own husband, assures friends and relatives that there is really nothing the matter with one but temporary nervous depression — a slight hysterical tendency — what is one to do?

My brother is also a physician, and also of high standing, and he says the same thing.

So I take phosphates or phosphites[2] — whichever it is, and tonics, and journeys, and air, and exercise, and am absolutely forbidden to "work" until I am well again.

Personally, I disagree with their ideas.

Personally, I believe that congenial[3] work, with excitement and change, would do me good.

But what is one to do?

I did write for a while in spite of them; but it *does* exhaust me a good deal — having to be so sly about it, or else meet with heavy opposition.

I sometimes fancy that in my condition if I had less opposition and more society and stimulus — but John says the very worst thing I can do is to think about my condition, and I confess it always makes me feel bad.

So I will let it alone and talk about the house.

The most beautiful place! It is quite alone, standing well back from the road, quite three miles from the village. It makes me think of English places that you read about, for there are hedges and walls and gates that lock, and lots of separate little houses for the gardeners and people.

There is a *delicious* garden! I never saw such a garden — large and shady, full of box-bordered paths, and lined with long grape-covered arbors with seats under them.

There were greenhouses, too, but they are all broken now.

---

[2] Phosphates were historically used as a remedy for depression and other nervous ailments, particularly in the 18th and 19th centuries, but were discontinued due to safety concerns and lack of efficacy.

[3] Pleasant or agreeable, especially suited to one's needs or nature.

There was some legal trouble, I believe, something about the heirs and co-heirs; anyhow, the place has been empty for years.

That spoils my ghostliness, I am afraid; but I don't care — there is something strange about the house — I can feel it.

I even said so to John one moonlight evening, but he said what I felt was a *draught*,[4] and shut the window.

I get unreasonably angry with John sometimes. I'm sure I never used to be so sensitive. I think it is due to this nervous condition.

But John says if I feel so I shall neglect proper self-control; so I take pains to control myself — before him, at least — and that makes me very tired.

I don't like our room a bit. I wanted one downstairs that opened on the piazza[5] and had roses all over the window, and such pretty old-fashioned chintz[6] hangings! but John would not hear of it.

He said there was only one window and not room for two beds, and no near room for him if he took another.

He is very careful and loving, and hardly lets me stir without special direction.

I have a schedule prescription for each hour in the day; he takes all care from me, and so I feel basely ungrateful not to value it more.

He said we came here solely on my account, that I was to have perfect rest and all the air I could get. "Your exercise depends on your strength, my dear," said he, "and your food somewhat on your appetite; but air you can absorb all the time." So we took the nursery, at the top of the house.

It is a big, airy room, the whole floor nearly, with windows that look all ways, and air and sunshine galore. It was nursery

---

[4] Draft; a current of cool air.

[5] In this context, the veranda or porch.

[6] A printed multicolored and glazed cotton fabric, usually of bright colors, typically used for curtains and upholstery.

ends p. 22

first and then playground and gymnasium, I should judge;
for the windows are barred for little children, and there are
rings and things in the walls.

The paint and paper look as if a boys' school had used it.
It is stripped off — the paper — in great patches all around
the head of my bed, about as far as I can reach, and in a great
place on the other side of the room low down. I never saw a
worse paper in my life.

One of those sprawling flamboyant patterns committing
every artistic sin.

It is dull enough to confuse the eye in following, pro-
nounced enough to constantly irritate, and provoke study,
and when you follow the lame, uncertain curves for a little
distance they suddenly commit suicide — plunge off at outra-
geous angles, destroy themselves in unheard-of contradictions.

The color is repellant, almost revolting; a smouldering,
unclean yellow, strangely faded by the slow-turning sunlight.

It is a dull yet lurid orange in some places, a sickly sulphur
tint in others.

No wonder the children hated it! I should hate it myself
if I had to live in this room long.

There comes John, and I must put this away — he hates
to have me write a word.

+

We have been here two weeks, and I haven't felt like writing
before, since that first day.

I am sitting by the window now, up in this atrocious nurs-
ery, and there is nothing to hinder my writing as much as I
please, save lack of strength.

John is away all day, and even some nights when his cases
are serious.

I am glad my case is not serious!

But these nervous troubles are dreadfully depressing.

John does not know how much I really suffer. He knows there is no *reason* to suffer, and that satisfies him.

Of course it is only nervousness. It does weigh on me so not to do my duty in any way!

I meant to be such a help to John, such a real rest and comfort, and here I am a comparative burden already!

Nobody would believe what an effort it is to do what little I am able — to dress and entertain, and order things.

It is fortunate Mary is so good with the baby. Such a dear baby!

And yet I *cannot* be with him, it makes me so nervous.

I suppose John never was nervous in his life. He laughs at me so about this wallpaper!

At first he meant to repaper the room, but afterward he said that I was letting it get the better of me, and that nothing was worse for a nervous patient than to give way to such fancies.

He said that after the wallpaper was changed it would be the heavy bedstead, and then the barred windows, and then that gate at the head of the stairs, and so on.

"You know the place is doing you good," he said, "and really, dear, I don't care to renovate the house just for a three months' rental."

"Then do let us go downstairs," I said, "there are such pretty rooms there."

Then he took me in his arms and called me a blessed little goose, and said he would go down cellar if I wished,[7] and have it whitewashed into the bargain.

But he is right enough about the beds and windows and things.

It is as airy and comfortable a room as anyone need wish,

---

[7] "Down cellar" is a regional American idiom, especially in New England, meaning "into the cellar." Its less common counterpart is "up attic."

ends p. 22

and, of course, I would not be so silly as to make him uncomfortable just for a whim.

I'm really getting quite fond of the big room, all but that horrid paper.

Out of one window I can see the garden, those mysterious deep-shaded arbors, the riotous old-fashioned flowers, and bushes and gnarly trees.

Out of another I get a lovely view of the bay and a little private wharf belonging to the estate. There is a beautiful shaded lane that runs down there from the house. I always fancy I see people walking in these numerous paths and arbors, but John has cautioned me not to give way to fancy in the least. He says that with my imaginative power and habit of story-making a nervous weakness like mine is sure to lead to all manner of excited fancies, and that I ought to use my will and good sense to check the tendency. So I try.

I think sometimes that if I were only well enough to write a little it would relieve the press of ideas and rest me.

But I find I get pretty tired when I try.

It is so discouraging not to have any advice and companionship about my work. When I get really well John says we will ask Cousin Henry and Julia down for a long visit; but he says he would as soon put fireworks in my pillowcase as to let me have those stimulating people about now.

I wish I could get well faster.

But I must not think about that. This paper looks to me as if it *knew* what a vicious influence it had!

There is a recurrent spot where the pattern lolls like a broken neck and two bulbous eyes stare at you upside-down.

I get positively angry with the impertinence of it and the everlastingness. Up and down and sideways they crawl, and those absurd, unblinking eyes are everywhere. There is one place where two breadths[8] didn't match, and the eyes go all up and down the line, one a little higher than the other.

I never saw so much expression in an inanimate thing before, and we all know how much expression they have! I used to lie awake as a child and get more entertainment and terror out of blank walls and plain furniture than most children could find in a toy-store.

I remember what a kindly wink the knobs of our big old bureau used to have, and there was one chair that always seemed like a strong friend.

I used to feel that if any of the other things looked too fierce I could always hop into that chair and be safe.

The furniture in this room is no worse than inharmonious, however, for we had to bring it all from downstairs. I suppose when this was used as a playroom they had to take the nursery things out, and no wonder! I never saw such ravages as the children have made here.

The wallpaper, as I said before, is torn off in spots, and it sticketh closer than a brother[9] — they must have had perseverance as well as hatred.

Then the floor is scratched and gouged and splintered, the plaster itself is dug out here and there, and this great heavy bed, which is all we found in the room, looks as if it had been through the wars.

But I don't mind it a bit — only the paper.

There comes John's sister. Such a dear girl as she is, and so careful of me! I must not let her find me writing.

She is a perfect, and enthusiastic housekeeper, and hopes for no better profession. I verily believe she thinks it is the writing which made me sick!

But I can write when she is out, and see her a long way off from these windows.

---

[8] In this context, the standard or definite width (from side to side) of the wallpaper.

[9] Allusion to Proverbs 18:24.

ends p. 22

There is one that commands the road, a lovely, shaded, winding road, and one that just looks off over the country. A lovely country, too, full of great elms and velvet meadows.

This wallpaper has a kind of sub-pattern in a different shade, a particularly irritating one, for you can only see it in certain lights, and not clearly then.

But in the places where it isn't faded, and where the sun is just so, I can see a strange, provoking, formless sort of figure, that seems to sulk about behind that silly and conspicuous front design.

There's sister on the stairs!

+

Well, the Fourth of July is over! The people are gone and I am tired out. John thought it might do me good to see a little company, so we just had mother and Nellie and the children down for a week.

Of course I didn't do a thing. Jennie sees to everything now.

But it tired me all the same.

John says if I don't pick up faster he shall send me to Weir Mitchell in the fall.[10]

But I don't want to go there at all. I had a friend who was in his hands once, and she says he is just like John and my brother, only more so!

Besides, it is such an undertaking to go so far.

I don't feel as if it was worthwhile to turn my hand over for anything, and I'm getting dreadfully fretful and querulous.[11]

I cry at nothing, and cry most of the time.

[10] Silas Weir Mitchell (1829–1914), American neurologist and author, considered the father of medical neurology, and famed for the "rest cure." Gilman was treated by Mitchell and subjected to his regimen, which enforced isolation and forbade intellectual activity.

[11] Given to habitually complaining.

Of course I don't when John is here, or anybody else, but when I am alone.

And I am alone a good deal just now. John is kept in town very often by serious cases, and Jennie is good and lets me alone when I want her to.

So I walk a little in the garden or down that lovely lane, sit on the porch under the roses, and lie down up here a good deal.

I'm getting really fond of the room in spite of the wallpaper. Perhaps *because* of the wallpaper.

It dwells in my mind so!

I lie here on this great immovable bed — it is nailed down, I believe — and follow that pattern about by the hour. It is as good as gymnastics, I assure you. I start, we'll say, at the bottom, down in the corner over there where it has not been touched, and I determine for the thousandth time that I *will* follow that pointless pattern to some sort of a conclusion.

I know a little of the principle of design, and I know this thing was not arranged on any laws of radiation, or alternation, or repetition, or symmetry, or anything else that I ever heard of.

It is repeated, of course, by the breadths, but not otherwise.

Looked at in one way each breadth stands alone, the bloated curves and flourishes — a kind of "debased Romanesque"[12] with *delirium tremens*[13] — go waddling up and down in isolated columns of fatuity.[14]

But, on the other hand, they connect diagonally, and the sprawling outlines run off in great slanting waves of optic horror, like a lot of wallowing seaweeds in full chase.

[12] Romanesque architecture flourished in Europe from the 10th–12th centuries and was marked by rounded arches and massive ornamentation. Gilman's narrator likens the wallpaper's bloated curves to a corrupted version of that style: grand forms degraded into grotesque decoration.

[13] A psychotic condition involving tremors, hallucinations, anxiety, and disorientation.

[14] Utter foolishness or stupidity.

ends p. 22

The whole thing goes horizontally, too, at least it seems so, and I exhaust myself in trying to distinguish the order of its going in that direction.

They have used a horizontal breadth for a frieze,[15] and that adds wonderfully to the confusion.

There is one end of the room where it is almost intact, and there, when the cross-lights fade and the low sun shines directly upon it, I can almost fancy radiation after all — the interminable grotesques seem to form around a common center and rush off in headlong plunges of equal distraction.

It makes me tired to follow it. I will take a nap, I guess.

+

I don't know why I should write this.

I don't want to.

I don't feel able.

And I know John would think it absurd. But I *must* say what I feel and think in some way — it is such a relief!

But the effort is getting to be greater than the relief.

Half the time now I am awfully lazy, and lie down ever so much.

John says I mustn't lose my strength, and has me take cod-liver oil and lots of tonics and things, to say nothing of ale and wine and rare meat.

Dear John! He loves me very dearly, and hates to have me sick. I tried to have a real earnest reasonable talk with him the other day, and tell him how I wish he would let me go and make a visit to Cousin Henry and Julia.

But he said I wasn't able to go, nor able to stand it after I got there; and I did not make out a very good case for myself, for I was crying before I had finished.

---

[15] A broad, decorative horizontal band or border, especially on a wall near the ceiling.

It is getting to be a great effort for me to think straight. Just this nervous weakness, I suppose.

And dear John gathered me up in his arms, and just carried me upstairs and laid me on the bed, and sat by me and read to me till it tired my head.

He said I was his darling and his comfort and all he had, and that I must take care of myself for his sake, and keep well.

He says no one but myself can help me out of it, that I must use my will and self-control and not let any silly fancies run away with me.

There's one comfort, the baby is well and happy, and does not have to occupy this nursery with the horrid wallpaper.

If we had not used it that blessed child would have! What a fortunate escape! Why, I wouldn't have a child of mine, an impressionable little thing, live in such a room for worlds.

I never thought of it before, but it is lucky that John kept me here after all. I can stand it so much easier than a baby, you see.

Of course I never mention it to them any more — I am too wise — but I keep watch of it all the same.

There are things in that paper that nobody knows but me, or ever will.

Behind that outside pattern the dim shapes get clearer every day.

It is always the same shape, only very numerous.

And it is like a woman stooping down and creeping about behind that pattern. I don't like it a bit. I wonder — I begin to think — I wish John would take me away from here!

✝

It is so hard to talk with John about my case, because he is so wise, and because he loves me so.

But I tried it last night.

ends p. 22

It was moonlight. The moon shines in all around, just as the sun does.

I hate to see it sometimes, it creeps so slowly, and always comes in by one window or another.

John was asleep and I hated to waken him, so I kept still and watched the moonlight on that undulating wallpaper till I felt creepy.

The faint figure behind seemed to shake the pattern, just as if she wanted to get out.

I got up softly and went to feel and see if the paper *did* move, and when I came back John was awake.

"What is it, little girl?" he said. "Don't go walking about like that — you'll get cold."

I thought it was a good time to talk, so I told him that I really was not gaining here, and that I wished he would take me away.

"Why darling!" said he, "our lease will be up in three weeks, and I can't see how to leave before.

"The repairs are not done at home, and I cannot possibly leave town just now. Of course if you were in any danger I could and would, but you really are better, dear, whether you can see it or not. I am a doctor, dear, and I know. You are gaining flesh and color, your appetite is better. I feel really much easier about you."

"I don't weigh a bit more," said I, "nor as much; and my appetite may be better in the evening, when you are here, but it is worse in the morning when you are away."

"Bless her little heart!" said he with a big hug; "she shall be as sick as she pleases! But now let's improve the shining hours by going to sleep, and talk about it in the morning!"

"And you won't go away?" I asked gloomily.

"Why, how can I, dear? It is only three weeks more and then we will take a nice little trip of a few days while Jennie is getting the house ready. Really, dear, you are better!"

"Better in body perhaps" — I began, and stopped short,

for he sat up straight and looked at me with such a stern, reproachful look that I could not say another word.

"My darling," said he, "I beg of you, for my sake and for our child's sake, as well as for your own, that you will never for one instant let that idea enter your mind! There is nothing so dangerous, so fascinating, to a temperament like yours. It is a false and foolish fancy. Can you not trust me as a physician when I tell you so?"

So of course I said no more on that score, and we went to sleep before long. He thought I was asleep first, but I wasn't — I lay there for hours trying to decide whether that front pattern and the back pattern really did move together or separately.

On a pattern like this, by daylight, there is a lack of sequence, a defiance of law, that is a constant irritant to a normal mind.

The color is hideous enough, and unreliable enough, and infuriating enough, but the pattern is torturing.

You think you have mastered it, but just as you get well under way in following, it turns a back somersault and there you are. It slaps you in the face, knocks you down, and tramples upon you. It is like a bad dream.

The outside pattern is a florid arabesque,[16] reminding one of a fungus. If you can imagine a toadstool in joints, an interminable string of toadstools, budding and sprouting in endless convolutions — why, that is something like it.

That is, sometimes!

There is one marked peculiarity about this paper, a thing nobody seems to notice but myself, and that is that it changes as the light changes.

When the sun shoots in through the east window — I

[16] A complex, ornamental style consisting of intricate intertwining leaf, flower, animal, or geometrical designs, originally found in Arabic or Moorish decoration.

ends p. 22

always watch for that first long, straight ray — it changes so quickly that I never can quite believe it.

That is why I watch it always.

By moonlight — the moon shines in all night when there is a moon — I wouldn't know it was the same paper.

At night in any kind of light, in twilight, candlelight, lamp-light, and worst of all by moonlight, it becomes bars! The outside pattern I mean, and the woman behind it is as plain as can be.

I didn't realize for a long time what the thing was that showed behind — that dim sub-pattern — but now I am quite sure it is a woman.

By daylight she is subdued, quiet. I fancy it is the pattern that keeps her so still. It is so puzzling. It keeps me quiet by the hour.

I lie down ever so much now. John says it is good for me, and to sleep all I can.

Indeed, he started the habit by making me lie down for an hour after each meal.

It is a very bad habit, I am convinced, for, you see, I don't sleep.

And that cultivates deceit, for I don't tell them I'm awake, — oh, no!

The fact is, I am getting a little afraid of John.

He seems very queer sometimes, and even Jennie has an inexplicable look.

It strikes me occasionally, just as a scientific hypothesis, that perhaps it is the paper!

I have watched John when he did not know I was look-ing, and come into the room suddenly on the most innocent excuses, and I've caught him several times *looking at the paper!* And Jennie too. I caught Jennie with her hand on it once.

She didn't know I was in the room, and when I asked her in a quiet, a very quiet voice, with the most restrained manner possible, what she was doing with the paper she turned around as if she had been caught stealing, and looked quite angry — asked me why I should frighten her so!

Then she said that the paper stained everything it touched, that she had found yellow smooches on all my clothes and John's, and she wished we would be more careful!

Did not that sound innocent? But I know she was studying that pattern, and I am determined that nobody shall find it out but myself!

+

Life is very much more exciting now than it used to be. You see I have something more to expect, to look forward to, to watch. I really do eat better, and am more quiet than I was.

John is so pleased to see me improve! He laughed a little the other day, and said I seemed to be flourishing in spite of my wallpaper.

I turned it off with a laugh. I had no intention of telling him it was *because* of the wallpaper — he would make fun of me. He might even want to take me away.

I don't want to leave now until I have found it out. There is a week more, and I think that will be enough.

+

I'm feeling ever so much better! I don't sleep much at night, for it is so interesting to watch developments; but I sleep a good deal in the daytime.

In the daytime it is tiresome and perplexing.

There are always new shoots on the fungus, and new shades of yellow all over it. I cannot keep count of them, though I have tried conscientiously.

ends p. 22

It is the strangest yellow, that wallpaper! It makes me think of all the yellow things I ever saw — not beautiful ones like buttercups, but old foul, bad yellow things.

But there is something else about that paper — the smell! I noticed it the moment we came into the room, but with so much air and sun it was not bad. Now we have had a week of fog and rain, and whether the windows are open or not, the smell is here.

It creeps all over the house.

I find it hovering in the dining-room, skulking in the parlor, hiding in the hall, lying in wait for me on the stairs.

It gets into my hair.

Even when I go to ride, if I turn my head suddenly and surprise it — there is that smell!

Such a peculiar odor, too! I have spent hours in trying to analyze it, to find what it smelled like.

It is not bad — at first, and very gentle, but quite the subtlest, most enduring odor I ever met.

In this damp weather it is awful. I wake up in the night and find it hanging over me.

It used to disturb me at first. I thought seriously of burning the house — to reach the smell.

But now I am used to it. The only thing I can think of that it is like is the *color* of the paper — a yellow smell!

There is a very funny mark on this wall, low down, near the mopboard.[17] A streak that runs round the room. It goes behind every piece of furniture, except the bed, a long, straight, even *smooch*, as if it had been rubbed over and over.

I wonder how it was done and who did it, and what they did it for. Round and round and round — round and round and round — it makes me dizzy!

+

---

[17] Baseboard, skirting, or trim.

I really have discovered something at last.

Through watching so much at night, when it changes so, I have finally found out.

The front pattern *does* move — and no wonder! The woman behind shakes it!

Sometimes I think there are a great many women behind, and sometimes only one, and she crawls around fast, and her crawling shakes it all over.

Then in the very bright spots she keeps still, and in the very shady spots she just takes hold of the bars and shakes them hard.

And she is all the time trying to climb through. But nobody could climb through that pattern — it strangles so; I think that is why it has so many heads.

They get through, and then the pattern strangles them off and turns them upside-down, and makes their eyes white!

If those heads were covered or taken off it would not be half so bad.

+

I think that woman gets out in the daytime!

And I'll tell you why — privately — I've seen her!

I can see her out of every one of my windows!

It is the same woman, I know, for she is always creeping, and most women do not creep by daylight.

I see her on that long shaded lane, creeping up and down. I see her in those dark grape arbors, creeping all around the garden.

I see her on that long road under the trees, creeping along, and when a carriage comes she hides under the blackberry vines.

I don't blame her a bit. It must be very humiliating to be caught creeping by daylight!

ends p. 22

I always lock the door when I creep by daylight. I can't do it at night, for I know John would suspect something at once.

And John is so queer now, that I don't want to irritate him. I wish he would take another room! Besides, I don't want anybody to get that woman out at night but myself.

I often wonder if I could see her out of all the windows at once.

But, turn as fast as I can, I can only see out of one at one time.

And though I always see her she *may* be able to creep faster than I can turn!

I have watched her sometimes away off in the open country, creeping as fast as a cloud shadow in a high wind.

+

If only that top pattern could be gotten off from the under one! I mean to try it, little by little.

I have found out another funny thing, but I shan't tell it this time! It does not do to trust people too much.

There are only two more days to get this paper off, and I believe John is beginning to notice. I don't like the look in his eyes.

And I heard him ask Jennie a lot of professional questions about me. She had a very good report to give.

She said I slept a good deal in the daytime.

John knows I don't sleep very well at night, for all I'm so quiet!

He asked me all sorts of questions, too, and pretended to be very loving and kind.

As if I couldn't see through him!

Still, I don't wonder he acts so, sleeping under this paper for three months.

It only interests me, but I feel sure John and Jennie are secretly affected by it.

+

Hurrah! This is the last day, but it is enough. John is to stay in town overnight, and won't be out until this evening.

Jennie wanted to sleep with me — the sly thing! but I told her I should undoubtedly rest better for a night all alone.

That was clever, for really I wasn't alone a bit! As soon as it was moonlight, and that poor thing began to crawl and shake the pattern, I got up and ran to help her.

I pulled and she shook, I shook and she pulled, and before morning we had peeled off yards of that paper.

A strip about as high as my head and half around the room.

And then when the sun came and that awful pattern began to laugh at me I declared I would finish it today!

We go away tomorrow, and they are moving all my furniture down again to leave things as they were before.

Jennie looked at the wall in amazement, but I told her merrily that I did it out of pure spite at the vicious thing.

She laughed and said she wouldn't mind doing it herself, but I must not get tired.

How she betrayed herself that time!

But I am here, and no person touches this paper but me — not *alive!*

She tried to get me out of the room — it was too patent![18] But I said it was so quiet and empty and clean now that I believed I would lie down again and sleep all I could; and not to wake me even for dinner — I would call when I woke.

So now she is gone, and the servants are gone, and the things are gone, and there is nothing left but that great

---

[18] Obvious.

ends p. 22

bedstead nailed down, with the canvas mattress we found on it.

We shall sleep downstairs tonight, and take the boat home tomorrow.

I quite enjoy the room, now it is bare again.

How those children did tear about here!

This bedstead is fairly gnawed!

But I must get to work.

I have locked the door and thrown the key down into the front path.

I don't want to go out, and I don't want to have anybody come in, till John comes.

I want to astonish him.

I've got a rope up here that even Jennie did not find. If that woman does get out, and tries to get away, I can tie her!

But I forgot I could not reach far without anything to stand on!

This bed will *not* move!

I tried to lift and push it until I was lame, and then I got so angry I bit off a little piece at one corner — but it hurt my teeth.

Then I peeled off all the paper I could reach standing on the floor. It sticks horribly and the pattern just enjoys it! All those strangled heads and bulbous eyes and waddling fungus growths just shriek with derision![19]

I am getting angry enough to do something desperate. To jump out of the window would be admirable exercise, but the bars are too strong even to try.

Besides I wouldn't do it. Of course not. I know well enough that a step like that is improper and might be misconstrued.

I don't like to *look* out of the windows even — there are so many of those creeping women, and they creep so fast.

I wonder if they all come out of that wallpaper as I did?

---

[19] Ridicule, mockery, or scorn.

But I am securely fastened now by my well-hidden rope — you don't get *me* out in the road there!

I suppose I shall have to get back behind the pattern when it comes night, and that is hard!

It is so pleasant to be out in this great room and creep around as I please!

I don't want to go outside. I won't, even if Jennie asks me to.

For outside you have to creep on the ground, and everything is green instead of yellow.

But here I can creep smoothly on the floor, and my shoulder just fits in that long smooch around the wall, so I cannot lose my way.

Why, there's John at the door!

It is no use, young man, you can't open it!

How he does call and pound!

Now he's crying for an axe.

It would be a shame to break down that beautiful door!

"John dear!" said I in the gentlest voice, "the key is down by the front steps, under a plantain leaf!"[20]

That silenced him for a few moments.

Then he said — very quietly indeed, "Open the door, my darling!"

"I can't," said I. "The key is down by the front door under a plantain leaf!"

And then I said it again, several times, very gently and slowly, and said it so often that he had to go and see, and he got it, of course, and came in. He stopped short by the door.

"What is the matter?" he cried. "For God's sake, what are you doing!"

I kept on creeping just the same, but I looked at him over my shoulder.

---

[20] Not the banana cousin, but the *Plantago* — a genus of flowering plants in the Plantaginaceae family, commonly called plantains or fleaworts. Often seen as a lawn and garden nuisance, but has many medicinal uses.

ends next p.

"I've got out at last," said I, "in spite of you and Jane! And I've pulled off most of the paper, so you can't put me back!"

Now why should that man have fainted? But he did, and right across my path by the wall, so that I had to creep over him every time!

Why I Wrote The Yellow Wallpaper?

Many and many a reader has asked that. When the story first came out, in *The New England Magazine* about 1891, a Boston physician made protest in *The Transcript*.[1] Such a story ought not to be written, he said; it was enough to drive anyone mad to read it.

Another physician, in Kansas I think, wrote to say that it was the best description of incipient insanity he had ever seen, and—begging my pardon—had I been there?

Now the story of the story is this:

For many years I suffered from a severe and continuous nervous breakdown tending to melancholia—and beyond. During about the third year of this trouble I went, in devout faith and some faint stir of hope, to a noted specialist in nervous diseases, the best known in the country. This wise man put me to bed and applied the rest cure, to which a still good physique responded so promptly that he concluded there was nothing much the matter with me, and sent me home with solemn advice to "live as domestic a life as far as possible," to "have but two hours' intellectual life a day," and "never to touch pen, brush, or pencil again as long as I lived." This was in 1887.

I went home and obeyed those directions for some three

---

[1] Perilous Stuff. (1892, April 8). *The Boston Evening Transcript*, A6. A facsimile can be found at the beginning of this book (page vi).

months, and came so near the border line of utter mental ruin that I could see over.

Then, using the remnants of intelligence that remained, and helped by a wise friend, I cast the noted specialist's advice to the winds and went to work again—work, the normal life of every human being; work, in which is joy and growth and service, without which one is a pauper and a parasite; ultimately recovering some measure of power.

Being naturally moved to rejoicing by this narrow escape, I wrote *The Yellow Wallpaper*,[2] with its embellishments and additions to carry out the ideal (I never had hallucinations or objections to my mural decorations) and sent a copy to the physician who so nearly drove me mad. He never acknowledged it.

The little book is valued by alienists and as a good specimen of one kind of literature. It has to my knowledge saved one woman from a similar fate—so terrifying her family that they let her out into normal activity and she recovered.

But the best result is this. Many years later I was told that the great specialist had admitted to friends of his that he had altered his treatment of neurasthenia[3] since reading *The Yellow Wallpaper*.

It was not intended to drive people crazy, but to save people from being driven crazy, and it worked.

---

[2] Note: the lack of hyphen here is carried over from the text as it was originally written/printed by Gilman in *The ForeRunner*.

[3] An obsolete technical term for a nervous breakdown.

Charlotte Perkins Gilman

HONORARY HEATHEN

It is the strangest yellow, that wallpaper!

* 9 7 9 8 9 0 0 7 5 0 0 1 9 *

"The following symbolic tale is from the pen of Hanns Heinz Ewers—the Edgar Allan Poe of Germany and one of the most notable authors writing in the German language. His fantastic imagination is perhaps best seen in the following story—unique, repelling, yet irresistible."   —*The International*

"If you like the weirdly horrible, read 'The Spider' by Hanns Heinz Ewers."   —*The Springfield News-Sun*

" . . . themes that would have warmed the heart of a Poe or Bierce. Take, for instance, Hannz Heinz Ewers' 'The Spider.' In this short-story the reader is treated to 15 minutes of chilled suspense that he will remember a long, long time."   —*The Buffalo Times*

"A tale as terrible as Edgar Allan Poe's most ghastly story."   —*The Fatherland*

"In the present generation German horror-fiction is most notably represented by Hanns Heinz Ewers, who brings to bear on his dark conceptions an effective knowledge of modern psychology . . . short stories like 'The Spider' contain distinctive qualities which raise them to a classic level."   —H.P. Lovecraft

"Ewers' horror is more utter than Poe's, both in atmosphere and in incident."   —Walter F. Kohn, *The New Republic*

"Of Ewers's short horror stories, the most famous is 'The Spider,' a splendid tale that presents . . . a narrative of spellbinding intensity. Ewers was fond of femme fatale creations, and in 'The Spider' he gives us one of the most nightmarish and original evil females in literature."   —Jack Sullivan, *Horror Literature*

So that
is what
LOVE
is like
Among
these
creatures....